Malian's Song

For information about permission to reproduce selections from this book, write to

PERMISSIONS
THE VERMONT FOLKLIFE CENTER
MASONIC HALL
3 COURT STREET, BOX 442
MIDDLEBURY, VERMONT 05753

LIBRARY OF CONGRESS | CATALOGING-IN-PUBLICATION DATA

Bruchac, Marge.
   Malian's song / by Marge Bruchac ; illustrated by William Maughan.— 1st ed.
      p. cm. — (Vermont Folklife Center children's book series)
   ISBN 0-916718-26-3 (alk. paper)
1. Abenaki Indians—History—Juvenile literature. 2. Abenaki Indians—Wars—Juvenile literature.
3. Saint Francis River (Québec)—History—Juvenile literature. 4. Rogers, Robert, 1731-1795—
Juvenile literature. 5. United States—History—French and Indian War, 1755-1763—Juvenile
literature.   I. Maughan, William, ill. II. Title. III. Series.
   E99.A13B795 2006
   974.004'9734—dc22

                                                                    2005017095

ISBN   0-916718-26-3
Printed in Singapore

Distributed by University Press of New England (UPNE)
1 Court Street, Lebanon, New Hampshire 03766

First Edition

Book Designer: R.W. Kosturko
Series Editor: Anita Silvey

10 9 8 7 6 5 4 3 2 1

A Vermont Folklife Center Book

Malian's Song

By Marge Bruchac

Illustrated by William Maughan

DISTRIBUTED BY UNIVERSITY PRESS OF NEW ENGLAND

HANOVER AND LONDON

My father, Simôn Obomsawin, woke me up early, before dawn. "Ho, Malian," he whispered, "*Nanibôsaid* lights the way."

We followed the moon's light down through the trees to the *Alsigontekw*, the river that runs near our village.

Simôn was teaching me how to talk to the fish people, the *namassaak*. "Think like water," he said. When he dropped his hand into the river, the *namassaak* swam right into it. I tried to do the same, but slipped and fell in. "Slow down, Malian. Sometimes you watch. Sometimes you catch."

My father was talking about hunting. "Remember last winter," he says to me, "when we caught *nôbamiskw*?"

My father, my mother Mali, and her mother Nokomis lived in one house with Maliazonis and me. We are related to almost everyone in the village. Nokomis says our family name, *Obomsawin*, means "one who leads or guides."

Nokomis was away that day. "French houses bring bad dreams," she had announced. "Time to build winter camp." I helped her pack her blankets and furs so that she and my mother could leave for Sibosek, the pine grove past the ravine.

When we opened the door, steam came out, as thick as smoke. My cousin, Maliazonis, was stirring a big pot of *yokeag*, corn porridge, over the fire. She dropped a sweet handful of dried blueberries and maple sugar into my bowl. "*Wlioni*, thank you," I said. Maliazonis is my favorite cousin.

I think maybe the *namassaak* were trying to warn me trouble was coming. But I did not yet know how to listen.

All I could hear that morning was my stomach. "The water monster is hungry," I said to my father. "It eats whoever is last," he said to me, laughing. Then he ran, up the hill to the village. My father was fast, but I reached the house first.

I remember that old beaver with thick silver and brown fur. We traded his pelt for a big silver broach and a dozen silver earrings. "Silver is good for protection," my father said. He stuck the broach on his hat, and put an earring in each of my ears.

Maliazonis was so excited that day she could hardly breathe. There was going to be a big feast at the Council House. "The hunters are coming home; the harvest is good; my cousin's cousin is getting married!" That meant the singing and dancing would go on a long time.

We spent all that afternoon preparing *skamôn*, corn, carrying many baskets to the stone houses. It was a lot of work.

"How many will this feed?" I asked my mother. She stretched out her arms, wide. More than enough for the winter.

By nightfall, I was worn out and needed to rest. My father went to the Council House, but Maliazonis promised to come back, later, to get me. So I went upstairs to sit on the foot of the bed, with my arms on the windowsill. All the houses were dark. I could hear the singing, from way down the street, so I sang along. The Friendship Dance was just starting when I fell asleep, still sitting in the window.

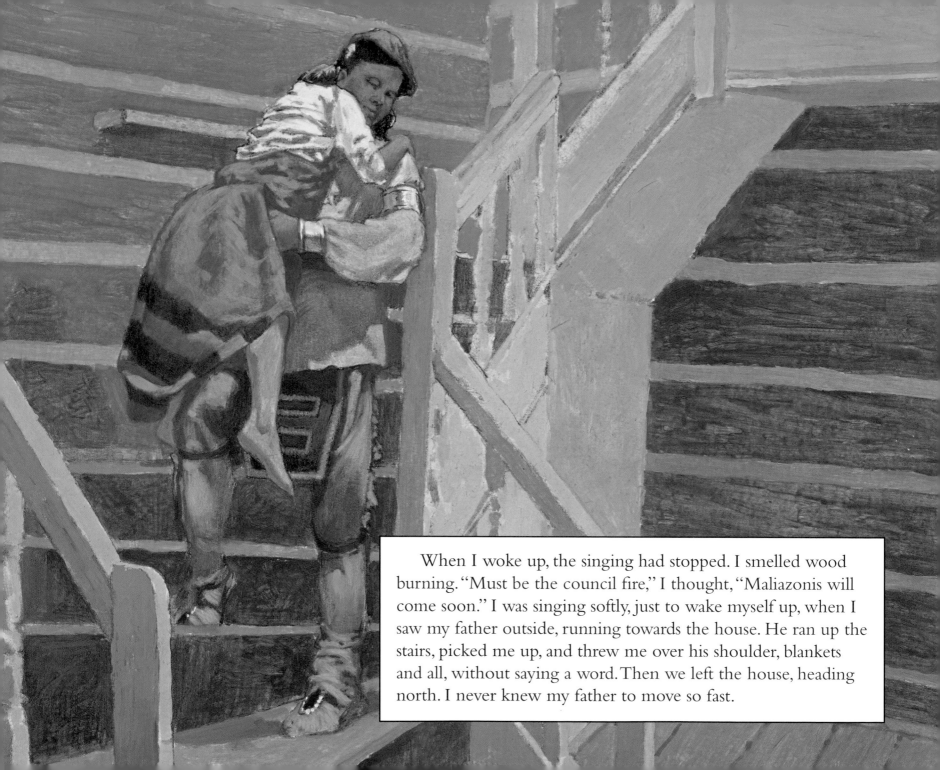

When I woke up, the singing had stopped. I smelled wood burning. "Must be the council fire," I thought, "Maliazonis will come soon." I was singing softly, just to wake myself up, when I saw my father outside, running towards the house. He ran up the stairs, picked me up, and threw me over his shoulder, blankets and all, without saying a word. Then we left the house, heading north. I never knew my father to move so fast.

When we got to the ravine, my father put me down and picked up a musket. He nodded towards the pine grove. "*Bemômahla*! Run, Malian!" But I did not run, not right away. Instead, I watched him slip through the trees as a speck of moonlight glinted off the silver on his hat. I watched until he was out of sight. Then I ran.

When I reached Sibosek, crowds of people were all huddled together at Nokomis' camp. Maliazonis grabbed me and hugged me tight. Then she told me the story.

At the Council House, there was much dancing. Maliazonis went out for air.

Then she heard a rustling noise in a bush, and saw a man hiding there. "*Idam, akwi sagez*," he said, "do not be afraid." "*Ndapsizak*, friend, *kwawimleba*, I've come to warn you."

Maliazonis thought he was joking until she saw the cut of his hair. "It was Samadagwis, scout for Madockawando, the White Devil!" she said. "He whispered '*Awanagiak*, strangers . . . come at dawn . . . burn village,' and then disappeared!"

Maliazonis took Samadagwis' warning straight to my father, who called the elders together. Some people did not believe her. But Simôn believed, and so did many of our neighbors.

They left the Council House early, walking slowly, and yawning, pretending nothing was wrong, in case anyone was watching.

We waited for a long time there, in the pine grove. Madockawando's men never found us, but their torches found our houses. All morning, the sky was bright with flames. Even the church burned.

When Father Roubaud, the Black Robe, returned, he fell to his knees and cried. More than thirty people had died. The food had been stolen. We found only a few handfuls of *skamón*, corn, scattered on the ground. Not enough for the winter.

My father never came back.

That winter, I stayed at Sibosek, but Maliazonis and many others moved away, back to the old places. My mother and grandmother blackened their faces, cut their hair, and never spoke a word until the snow melted. I made a Lonesome Song:

"*Nziwaldam, nziwaldam, anakwika ndodana*
I am lonesome; I am lonesome; our village grows up to trees
Malian pihta oziwaldam, nda tômô widôba
Malian she is very lonesome; there is no friend anywhere."

By *benibagos*, leaf-falling time, we built a new small house where the old one had been. After a long time, I married and had children. When my children had children, my cousin Maliazonis came back to Odanak to live with me.

Together, we tell the young ones stories about the old village. When they ask us how so many people escaped from Madockawando, we tell them about the warnings. My little granddaughter, Mali Msadoques, will carry these stories around after I get too old to talk. After she has walked on, someone else will carry them for us. As long as we have the stories, all our relatives will still be with us.

Nemikwaldamnana. We remember.

The Facts Behind Rogers' Raid on the St. Francis Abenaki, October 4, 1759

Malian's Song shows us the Abenaki perspective on the English attack of October 4, 1759. The fishing scene is fictional, but the other parts of this book—the silver broach, the Council House dance, Samadagwis' warning, the hiding place at Sibosek, the attack, Malian's rescue, the burning village, and the lonesome song—are all true. This book is based on the memories of those events preserved in the oral traditions of the Obomsawin and Msadoques families.

Malian's village, Odanak, was situated on the St. Francis River, near the St. Lawrence, north of Montreal. In the late 1600s, Jesuit missionaries built a Catholic church at St. Francis and offered the Abenaki protection under the colony of New France. The St. Francis Abenaki community included many Native refugees from New England—*Sokoki, Pocumtuck, Woronoco, Cowass, Pequawket,* and others—who had been forced out of their homelands by English colonists. These groups, as part of the "St. Francis Abenaki," then allied with the French soldiers to resist further English invasions.

By 1759, several hundred *Wôbanakiak* (Abenaki Indian people) were living in a village built around a central square, with a church and a large Council House. Simôn and his daughter Malian Obomsawin lived in a two-story house. Most of the 51 houses at Odanak were English or French-style wood-frame homes; three were built of stone.

General Jeffrey Amherst, commander of British troops in the American colonies, ordered the attack on the Abenaki village, with instructions "that no women or children are killed or hurt." Major Robert Rogers was commissioned to lead a group of 118 English regulars (volunteers and provincial soldiers) and 24 Stockbridge Mohican Indians north up Lake Champlain towards St. Francis. The attack was delayed when Rogers' boats were discovered, and scuttled, by the Missisquoi Abenaki at Missisquoi Bay.

Robert Rogers' journal recorded the attack of October 4, 1759, as follows:

"At half hour before sunrise I surprised the town when they were all fast asleep . . . A little after sunrise I set fire to

all their houses except three in which there was corn that I reserved for the use of the party . . . About seven o'clock in the morning the affair was completely over, in which time we had killed at least two hundred Indians."

In fact, only 32 Abenaki died, most of them women and children. Nearly 200 survived. Rogers may have exaggerated his account to cover his own losses, since 43 rangers—more than half of his men—died during the retreat. The Jesuit Father Joseph Antoine Roubaud returned to St. Francis that afternoon to find:

"Most of the village was burned to ashes including my house . . . Ten men and twenty-two women and infants [dead]. I gathered my savages and the next day we pursued the assailants. Because of lack of provisions, Major Rogers divided his party. My savages took prisoners and destroyed three-fourths of the detachment."

There are many Abenaki oral traditions that recall the raid. Some recalled premonitions, and signs, including seeing wood chips floating on the St. Francis River, from the rafts Rogers' men built to replace their lost boats. Others describe the pursuit of the raiders. Maliazonis' story reveals exactly why so many Abenaki people survived the attack that destroyed their village: one of Rogers' Stockbridge Mohican scouts gave a warning.

Malian Obomsawin passed the oral tradition on to her granddaughter, Mali Msadoques, who passed it on to her young niece, Elvine Obomsawin. In October of 1959, 200 years after the attack, Elvine shared some of her family memories with the ethnologist Gordon Day. When Gordon Day published several of these Abenaki accounts in an article titled "Rogers' Raid in Indian Tradition," historians were amazed. Elvine Obomsawin's granddaughter, Jeanne Brink, was awestruck, since she only knew her grandmother as a basketmaker, not as an oral historian. In 2001, the Vermont Folklife Center recorded Jeanne Brink's recollections of Elvine in an interview.

"I just saw her as this lady that . . . was Indian, that talked Indian to her sister and her brother . . . [then] I realized that she knew this amazing piece of history, Abenaki history. That no ethnologist or historian or non-Native

person had ever heard the Abenaki version . . . she got the story from her aunt, who got it from her grandmother, who was a little girl at the time of Rogers' Raid in 1759. So that shows me that it was the women who kept the oral tradition alive. And it usually skipped a generation."

During the early to mid-1900s, Abenaki traditions were largely ignored by white people who looked down on Indians. Abenaki elders tried to protect their children from prejudice by not teaching them their Native language, and not talking about their history. Some, especially those who lived in New England, still lived in fear that one day, the descendants of Rogers' Rangers would come to finish them off.

Today, Jeanne Brink, and many other Abenaki people, refuse to live in fear anymore. They are finally speaking the truth about the past, and sharing their knowledge with anyone who is willing to listen. Malian's song is just one tradition, out of many powerful stories about history and memory and family.

Bibiography

Jeanne Brink. Oral History Interview with Jane Beck and Greg Sharrow. Vermont Folklife Center. October 31, 2001.

Joseph Bruchac. *The Winter People.* New York, NY: Dial Books 2002.

Gordon Day. "Rogers' Raid in Indian Tradition," in *Historical New Hampshire.* Vol. XVII June 1962, pp. 3-17.

Gordon Day. *The Identity of the Saint Francis Indians.* Canadian Ethnology Service Paper No. 71. Ottawa, Ontario: National Museums of Canada 1981.

Burt Garfield Loescher. *The History of Rogers' Rangers.* Vol. 4. Bowie, MD: Heritage Books 2002.

Robert Rogers. *Journals of Major Robert Rogers* (1765) reprinted Corinth, NY: Corinth Books 1961.

An Abenaki glossary, portions of the Gordon Day interview in both English and Abenaki, and other related material about Malian's Song *can be found at www.vermontfolklifecenter.org.*